I'll Meet You in Your Dreams

WRITTEN BY
Jessica Young

ILLUSTRATED BY
Rafael López

LB
Little, Brown and Company
New York Boston

Each evening when the sun has set,
as nighttime casts a starry net,
I'll hitch a ride on moonbeams
and meet you in your dreams.

Adventures wait for you and me.
Close your eyes, and see.
First...

you'll be my little bumblebee.
I'll feed you sips of nectar tea.
We'll snuggle in a flower

until it starts to shower.
Then…

you'll be a mouse and I'll be a mole.
We'll dig a dry and cozy hole
and build a fort for two

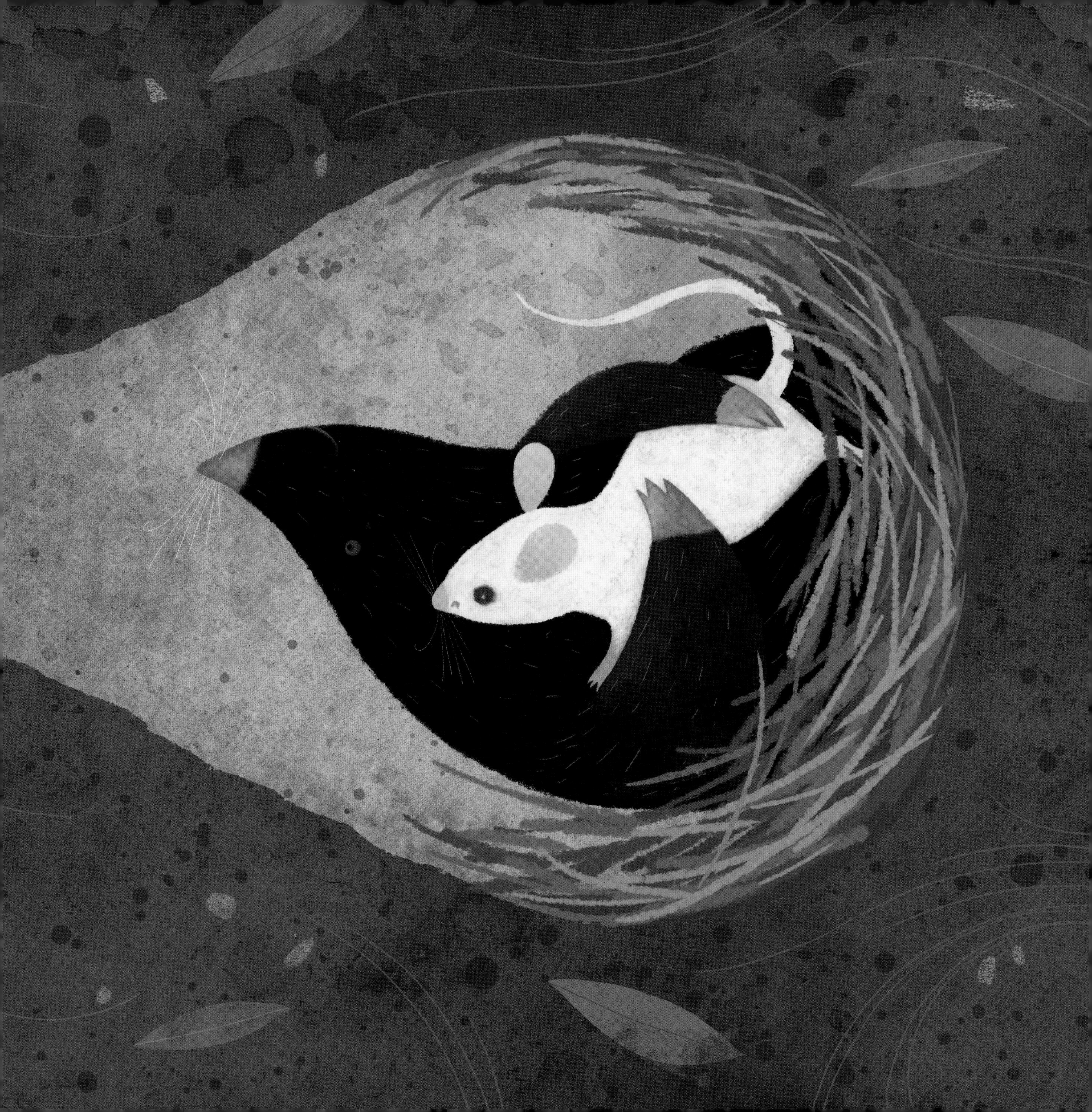

until the rain is through.
Then...

you'll be a knight and I'll be a horse.
We'll race along a rainbow's course
to castles in the sky

until it's time to fly.
Then...

you'll be an eagle and I'll be a hawk.
When soft winds sing and treetops rock,
we'll spread our wings and soar

until we reach the shore.
Then...

I'll be a lighthouse and you'll be a ship.
You'll set your sails and take a trip
across the briny sea

till you blow home to me.
Then…

we'll be two stars twinkling bright.
Side by side, we'll shine our light
and guide each other's way

till darkness turns to day.
Then…

you'll be you and I'll be me.
You'll travel places I can't see—

but as you grow, I'll be with you,
for every step, your whole life through.
And where the future gleams…

I'll meet you in your dreams.

To my family and all families —JY

We are the stories of those who came before us —RL

ABOUT THIS BOOK

The illustrations for this book were done in watercolor, gouache, acrylic, pencil, ink, and digital media. This book was edited by Andrea Spooner and designed by Saho Fujii. The production was supervised by Patricia Alvarado, and the production editor was Marisa Finkelstein. The text was set in Oneleigh Bold, and the display type is Galea.

 ★ Little, Brown and Company ★ Hachette Book Group ★ 1290 Avenue of the Americas, New York, NY 10104 ★ Visit us at LBYR.com ★ First Edition: March 2021 ★ Little, Brown and Company is a division of Hachette Book Group, Inc. ★ The Little, Brown name and logo are trademarks of Hachette Book Group, Inc. ★ The publisher is not responsible for websites (or their content) that are not owned by the publisher. ★ Library of Congress Cataloging-in-Publication Data ★ Names: Young, Jessica (Jessica E.), author. | López, Rafael, 1961– illustrator. ★ Title: I'll meet you in your dreams / written by Jessica Young; illustrated by Rafael López. ★ Other titles: I will meet you in your dreams ★ Description: First edition. | New York: Little, Brown and Company, 2021. | Audience: Ages 4–8. | Summary: "A child and parent journey through life together—always remembering that even if the other is far away they can meet in their dreams" —Provided by publisher. ★ Identifiers: LCCN 2019040244 | ISBN 9780316453288 (hardcover) ★ Subjects: CYAC: Stories in rhyme. | Parent and child—Fiction. | Dreams—Fiction. ★ Classification: LCC PZ8.3.Y7873 Ill 2021 | DDC [E]—dc23 ★ LC record available at https://lccn.loc.gov/2019040244 ★ ISBN 978-0-316-45328-8 ★ PRINTED IN CHINA ★ APS ★ 10 9 8 7 6 5 4 3 2 1